THE SMITHS OF 57TH STREET

DEETYA JAGADEESH

Made with ♥ on the Notion Press Platform
www.notionpress.com

Contents

Acknowledgements

First and foremost, I would like to thank my parents, my favorite people in the whole world, for encouraging me and providing their full support throughout my writing journey.

Next, I would like to mention my friends at school, to whom I've narrated *this* story bit by bit and the next ones too and thank them for their support and help.

My favorite authors, my inspiration, as I have them to thank for providing me with such good literature. A few of them being Enid Blyton, Karina Yan Glaser, Rick Riordan, Ilika Ranjan, J K Rowling, David Walliams, Sudha Murthy, Lauren Wolk and Jeff Kinney.

My school, for providing me with the basic education without which I would not be able to read or write. Also, all my teachers who have put in a lot of effort to make sure I learnt my basics.

I am also acknowledging the publisher who agreed to publish my book, as without them, this story wouldn't have gone anywhere.

Last but not least, I acknowledge myself for not giving up on the story no matter how terrible I thought it was.

ONE

In the middle of a small community in Brooklyn, New York lived the Smith family in a humble brownstone with their assortment of pets including a dog, one cat, one kitten, two rabbits, a fish and a parrot.

The brownstone was located on the 57th Street of Brooklyn, opposite to the local church which had an empty plot next to it. On either side of the brownstone were two double decker houses. One of them had a small weathervane on top, which spun crazily every time there was the slightest of breezes. Just a few blocks away from the Smiths' brownstone lived their friends, all scattered in various directions as if the winds had chosen the location for their houses. 57th Street was connected to one main road in Brooklyn and was always bustling with activity from ten in the morning to seven in the evening.

The eldest of the five Smith kids was Harry, a boy of fourteen years of age resembling their father with short cropped blonde hair, blue eyes and a handsome face. Excellent at basketball, he was valued very much in his school. Next was Hannah, a girl of twelve years of age resembling their *mother* with light brown eyes and long brown hair that fell over her shoulders like a waterfall. She had been taking piano classes for over six years now and she was famous in her locality for the marvelous songs that she could play. Next came the twins, Peter and Molly, both eight years of age. Peter had short, spiky brown hair with brilliant blue eyes and a charming smile. He played football so well that everyone wanted him on their team. Molly had greyish-blonde hair which was wavy, unlike Hannah's straight waterfall. She kept her hair short, in a bob more specifically, to avoid the puzzle of braiding them each morning. She had brown eyes and was the topper in her class, however, she was extremely shy. The youngest of the five Smith kids was Anne. A cute girl at six years, she was a perfect blend of their parents, her skin tone perfect, chocolate brown hair and hazel eyes. Known for her impressive drawings, Anne was adored by all.

The Smiths had seven pets in total. The dog belonging to Molly was named Brownie, the tabby cat owned by Harry and Hannah was known as Fluffy, the two rabbits owned by Peter were named PB and J, the fish, the parrot and the kitten owned by Anne were named Dory, Pat and Queenie, respectively. What with all the pets, every time a Smith was asked to draw up their family tree, they ended up making an enormously huge one for it *had* to include all the pets as they were a part of the family too.

Back home from school for the Easter holidays, the Smith kids were having the time of their life. All was well until one day, Mrs. Smith came into the living room where the kids were sprawled, followed by Mr. Smith.

"Kids!", Mama said." Listen up! Papa and I have discussed this matter and we would like to tell you that---------"

"Wait!", Harry interrupted. "I do hope it's not another kid. Man, am I tired of looking after the youngsters in the family."

Hannah rolled her eyes. "*I* do most of the looking after, you know?"

They all laughed.

"Actually Harry,", Mama said. "It is, fortunately, not another sibling. You all know how much I love baking, right?"

Their mom, a professional baker, was known very well not only on 57th Street but many others too. Now, each of the five Smith kids looked up at their mom and tried to see if they could fathom anything out of her excited and shining face.

Mama sighed almost impatiently when she saw her kids staring blankly up at her. "How about I decide to open a bakery of my own and surprise the entire locality of Brooklyn with my extraordinary baking skills?", she said, her eyes shining.

They all laughed at the hidden humor in Mama's lines and chorused, "Nice!"

"Mama wants a bakery! Mama wants a bakery!", Pat said. Everybody laughed again. Then Hannah spoke up.

"Where are you going to open it though?"

Papa smiled uncertainly at her. "We haven't found the right place yet."

"Then how are you so sure", Molly said. "That you will get the bakery?"

Mama glared at her. "Because I'm strong-minded. And I know that when I want a bakery, I will *get* a bakery."

The kids 'oohed' at this punch line making Mama swell up incredibly with pride.

"Do you want us to help?", Harry asked.

"Not really", Papa said. "Although... we may need you for something."

"Hmm...", Hannah said. Then after a pause she asked," Can I go to Jane's house?"

Jane Hope was Hannah's best friend.

"Go", Mama sighed. "And no need to ask Harry, you can go to Mike's house", spotting Harry trying to turn on his 'puppy eyes.'

Michael Turner *(or Mike as he was known)* was Harry's best friend.

After Hannah and Harry left, Papa said," Peter, get a football. Let's play. And Molly, you and Anne help your mother in the kitchen."

"Okay", they chorused.

TWO

Hannah walked into Jane's house.

"Hi Jane!"

"Hey Hannah! Wanna see this experiment or try on a dress?"

Hannah laughed. Her friend was both a science nerd and her wardrobe manager.

"Dress!", Hannah said

" I knew it!", Jane said. Handing her a long black gown with frills, she said, "Here! Try this on!"

Hannah slipped it on and Jane zipped her up.

"Wow! Wow! WOW!", Jane squealed. "You look like a queen!"

"Really?", asked Hannah, gliding over to the nearest mirror. Looking at herself, she gasped. Her moment of peace was rudely shattered with a volley of shouts and screams of laughter from the next house.

"Ugh!", Jane said. "Mike just ***cannot*** keep quiet despite the number of times I have told him to!!"

"Oh!", Hannah said. "It's okay Jane. I'll go talk to them."

So, Hannah still wearing the gown stormed out of Jane's house and walked into Mike's bursting the door open. She saw the two boys, sprawled on the living room carpet, heaving with laughter. But as soon as they saw her, they straightened up.

"Hey Hannah", Mike said. "Haven't seen you for a while."

Hannah smiled. "Hey Mike. Good to see you too. Just do me a favor and keep your voices down, will you?"

"Yeah", Mike said. "Sure."

"Thanks", Hannah said.

"Wow!", Mike said, once she was gone. "She grew up gorgeous."

Harry smiled." Well, yeah. She did."

"Hey...uh... you know the end of term party in our school?"

"Yeah?"

"Well, do you think I should ask her?"

"Probably. You are her friend after all. I suggest you give it a try."

"Thanks Harry", Mike said. "You're the best."

Meanwhile, Hannah and Jane had been squabbling over a nail polish set. They both wanted Rose Pink and would not let each other have it.

"I love this color Jane", Hannah whined. "Give it to me. Please?"

"Hannah", Jane said. "It's *my* set."

"Alright", Hannah grumbled. "But make it quick."

"Ball! Ball! Ball incoming!", Pat said, who was perched on the window sill watching Mama, Molly and Anne prepare lunch.

Mama looked up from her recipe book just in time and she ducked as the ball flew over her head and banged into the kitchen wall.

"HEY! Watch where you kick that ball!", Mama said, as she picked it up and threw it out the window. "Gross", she muttered, wiping flecks of mud and dirt off her hands and onto the apron she was wearing.

"Sorry!", said Papa and Peter.

"Okay. Molly, have you got everything?"

"Yes Mama. I have the eggs, butter, flour and the sugar."

"And I", Anne said. "Have the tray, the butter paper, the beater and the oven is preheated."

"Righto! Let's get this started them."

As the sun slowly rose in the sky, the neighborhood bustled with activity. The smell of food had wafted all the way to both Jane's and Mike's house and Hannah and Harry knew it was time to go.

"Bye Jane.", Hannah said." I gotta go for lunch. Hey, how about you come over to my place?"

"I wish", Jane said. "But my dad has an off and he's coming over."

Jane's dad being a veterinary doctor was extremely busy owing to the fact that his pet clinic was the only one closest to all the residents of Brooklyn. He visited Jane and her mom on weekends and Jane treasured these days. She now watched as Hannah stood up, brushing her jeans.

"Hmm... Okay then. Bye!", Hannah said.

Meanwhile, Mike had been finishing his comic with Harry.

"Hey...uh... I gotta go, okay?", Harry said. "I'll catch you later."

"What?!", Mike said. "Oh! It's lunch time, isn't it? Okay. Bye!"

Hannah and Harry caught up at the front door and as they went in, they saw Mama setting the table and Papa and Peter coming down after a wash.

"Hannah! Harry! Go freshen up and come fast.", Mama said seeing them enter.

After lunch, a marvelous one at that with roast chicken, salad, boiled potatoes in their jackets, cookies and an enormous jug of cream, the kids went up to the DR *(Decision Room)* to plan Mama's bakery as per Hannah's request.

"So", Harry said, once they were inside. "What do you think we should do?"

Hannah looked surprised. "I don't have a plan. *We* need to form one."

"Okay.", Peter said. "First, we should look for-------------"

But whatever he was going to say was drowned by a loud shout from downstairs followed by squawks and a volley of barks and everything was forgotten as the five Smith kids raced downstairs.

THREE

"Mama! Papa!", Anne cried. "Where are you?"

"Here, honey", came Mama's reassuring voice.

All five of them raced into the kitchen and they were just in time to see the mess.

"Goodness me, Mama!", Peter exclaimed. "What have you been doing?"

There were eggshells on the floor, flour all over the slabs, black thingamajigs in the oven, egg yolk and butter on the wall and icing everywhere. To top this, there were tins on the floor, upturned bowls everywhere and broken, *broken* plates in the sink.

"Brownie is a bad dog! Brownie is a bad dog!", Pat squawked causing Molly to shake her fist at him angrily, making him fly into the living room, dropping feathers everywhere.

"And what does Pat mean?", Anne asked.

"Pat means to say that the cause of this ***extremely*** big mess is Brownie", Mama explained, getting to her feet.

"How?", Molly asked. "He is trained extremely well."

"Well Molly", Mama said angrily. "Maybe you *forgot* to train him to ***NOT*** chase Fluffy?"

"Oh.", Molly said. "I'm sorry."

"Well, just do me a favor and *TAKE BROWNIE **OUT!***"

So, it was a very subdued Molly with an even more subdued Brownie that went out of the house.

"Yikes!", Hannah said. "Let me help you with that Mama."

"Thanks Hannah", Mama said as Hannah picked up a cloth and started wiping the slabs and the walls. Harry followed suit, picking up the broken pieces of the plates and putting them in the bin. Anne helped by taking the burnt whatever-it-was out of the oven and putting it in the bin while Peter went out to comfort Molly.

When Peter went out, Hannah whispered, "Mama, are the cakes for Molly and Peter's birthday done?"

"Yes", Mama whispered back. "I just need some time to clean this up."

With four pairs of hands working at the mess, it was cleaned in less than twenty minutes. Then the doorbell rang and Harry opened it. He saw Mike, Jane, Molly's friends, their relatives and a few other respected people in their community. Beckoning them inside, he gestured for them to hide.

"Mama?", Molly called. "I'm sorry for what happened. Can I come inside?"

Hearing that, the Smiths quickly hid themselves too.

"Yes, honey!", Mama said, from her place behind the couch.

Molly came in, followed by Peter and they stared around the house but could not catch a glimpse of any of their siblings. Just when they were about to call out, everybody jumped out of their hiding places and yelled, "Happy Birthday!"

"WOW!", Peter and Molly said. "Thank you so much!"

And then Molly spotted him. She ran all the way to the front door to tackle her best friend Oliver, in a bear hug.

"Oliver!", she squealed. "You made it!!"

"Of course", he said. "Which best friend forgets a birthday?"

After all the gifts were handed out, the cakes were cut and everybody had the time of their life. Pat kept on squawking "Happy Happy Happy Birthday" until somebody got mad and chased him all around the house.

After the party was over, everyone went home and the five kids raced upstairs to the DR to discuss their bakery plans.

"Right", said Hannah, plonking herself down on the couch in the DR. "About that plan----"

"Hannah!", Mama hollered suddenly. "Harry! You two need to be in Rock 'n' Roll café in ten minutes! Mike called so get dressed. And

FAST!"

They all grumbled as Hannah and Harry got up, ran into their rooms and began to change.

Two minutes later they left the house.

Ten minutes later, they were at the café.

A second later, Mama's car sped away.

"Like I was saying", Peter said. "We should research for some places nearby that will be suitable for Mama's bakery."

Although Hannah and Harry were at Rock 'n' Roll café, the three younger Smith siblings were brainstorming on ideas for the bakery.

"Good idea", Molly said. She got Harry's laptop out and started typing. Everyone waited. After thirty minutes of research, Molly said, "Well, I can't find any. Maybe we should take a walk and see what we find."

"I think that is a great idea.", Peter said. Anne got to her feet but Molly pulled her back. "And where do you think you're going?"

"Down", Anne said but Molly made her stay and play.

"Mike!", Harry said, running to greet his friend and almost knocking over a cup of coffee in his hurry.

"Hi Harry", Mike said. "Hi Hannah."

"Hi. Um... my mom said *you* called us here Mike", Hannah said. "Why?"

Harry, sensing that Mike wanted to talk privately, said, "I'm going to go and talk to Jason. Anybody want anything?"

"Nope."

After Harry left, Mike and Hannah faced each other and for a minute, there was absolute silence. Mike took in the way Hannah's hair moved in the slightest of winds, her eyes and her calm and steady expression. Hannah took in Mike's handsome but cute face, reassuring eyes and a rather hopeful expression. Finally, Hannah gathered all of her willpower and snapped out of it.

"So", she said. "You were saying?"

"Oh!", Mike said. "Uh... you're in seventh, right?"

"Yeah."

"You ever been to a party? You know, other than *birthday parties*?"

"Yeah. With my friends."

"Just a casual question, who are your closest friends?"

"Well, everyone in my family, Jane and you.", Hannah said. "Although Mike, I wish you'd get to the point."

"Okay.", Mike said. "I want to invite you to the end of term party in our school. Will you come with me?"

"Mike... I... I don't know", she said, completely taken by surprise.

"It's okay", he said. "Just take your time."

"Well... how about I tell you in two days' time?"

"Okay.", Mike said, although his face fell. "Great."

Harry came up and said, "Hannah, we should leave."

But before Hannah could reply, Mike said, "Harry, I invited your sister to go with me to the end of term party in our school. What do you think?"

Harry smiled and tried to look as though he was hearing about this for the very first time. "Um... wow! Yeah, um... that's very nice of you, Mike."

"Thanks", Mike said, grinning. There was a moment of awkward pause.

Then Hannah said, "Okay Harry, let's leave. Bye Mike."

"Bye!"

Hannah came home and changed. Afterwards, she and Harry sat along with Molly, Peter and Anne to review on the research that they had done. They all agreed to take a walk to the nearby streets the next day and then Mama called.

"Dinner!"

"Mama!", Molly said. "We've just eaten *enormous* slices of cake!"

"Excuses!", Mama said. "It's taco night today. Courtesy of two birthdays. Anyone who is feeling stuffed is more than welcome to sit this out!"

"Don't you even think about it Mama!", yelled the kids as they raced each other downstairs.

After dinner as the last member of the family finally headed upstairs for the night, the brownstone creaked loudly, embracing them for another night.

"Goodnight Hannah", said Molly and Anne.

But Hannah was already asleep.

FOUR

(DAYS FOR BAKERY:8)

Molly was the first one to wake up the next morning and she headed downstairs to feed the pets. Brownie greeted her, licking her ankles.

"Hello Brownie", she cooed as she scooped out a bowl filled with biscuits. "Bon Appetite!"

She went around the hall, feeding the fish, stroking the cats who purred in their sleep and kissing the rabbits on their nose. Careful not to wake Pat who was perched on the kitchen windowsill, she got herself a glass of water. Slowly, the next Smith member awoke and then the next and the brownstone creaked happily as the family descended downstairs.

After breakfast, all the siblings got ready, told Mama that they were going to take a walk, put Brownie on his leash and went outside, each Smith already imagining the bakery they were going to give their mother.

The Smiths were A+ walkers and they could walk for miles without getting tired. They took a walk around the nearby streets and when they reached 50th Street, Brownie began to tug on his leash.

"Brownie!", Molly said, clearly exasperated. "What is the matter?"

He began to strain and Molly, afraid that he would choke, let him off his leash. At once, he bounded off, chasing a few squirrels in the trees. Molly watched him, reproachfully. Hannah put an arm on her shoulder.

"Hey", Hannah said. "Let's look around for a while."

They walked around and came to a place where Brownie was standing. His hackles were up but he wasn't growling. He was facing an old, rundown, out-of-shape hut. When he saw Molly, he turned around but his hackles didn't go down.

"Come on Brownie", Molly said. "Let's go home. I don't like the look of that hut."

They headed home and Hannah spoke on the way back.

"Mama's birthday is like a week away. Do you think we can do this?"

Hannah half expected an outbreak at this but to her surprise, nobody spoke.

"What does Mama's birthday have to do with this?", Peter asked, after a moment's silence.

"Oh. Right.", Hannah said, clasping a hand to her forehead. "You don't know. I was just thinking about how nice it would be if we gave her the bakery she wants for her birthday."

"That", Anne said. "Would be the best birthday gift ever."

After dinner, Harry called a meeting and the others found out that he had borrowed Papa's laptop.

When Peter gave him a strange look, he said, "It has much more access than mine."

He researched and after one hour, he put the laptop down, clearly frustrated.

"WHY", he bellowed. "AREN'T THERE ANY PROPETIES FOR SALE??!!"

"Calm down", Hannah said, putting an arm around him. "We'll find something."

That night as they headed upstairs to sleep, Harry asked Hannah if she would stay back for a bit as he needed to talk to her about something.

"Uh... okay?", she said.

Once they were in the room, Harry said, “Did you and Mike fix things out?”

“Kind of”, Hannah replied. “I thought that it would be nice to go with him cause he’s really sweet, you know?”

“Hmm...”, Harry said. “See, I need to find someone too. I feel jea—jealous that you and Mike have each other.”

Hannah laughed. “That’s all?”, she said. “Fine. I’ll give you some names and you just tell me which one.”

“Okay.”

“Meg?”

“No?”

“Penelope?”

“Yuck!”

“Meg? The other one, you know, Margaret.”

“Meh.”

“Kathy.”

“Grr...”, Harry said.

“Jane?”

“Jeez, I was waiting for you to get there. Duh! Can you tell her, please?”

“No. Harry, *you* need to ask her to the party, not *me*.”

“Fine”, he said. “It won’t go well but... just fine.”

FIVE

(DAYS FOR BAKERY:7)

The next morning, the Smiths got up early. Molly was the last and when she came out of her room, she saw a long line of her siblings waiting for the bathroom. Hannah and Harry looked tired while Anne was hopping about on one foot. Mama was in the kitchen and Papa was helping her.

"I need to go!!", Anne squealed, hopping faster than ever.

Hannah banged on the door. It opened and Peter came out, carrying a copy of David Walliam's 'Bad Dad'.

"Peter!", Harry scolded. "No reading in the bathroom."

"Ugh!", Peter said. "You guys interrupted me in the MIDDLE of the climax!!"

"No reading in the bathroom", Hannah said in her I'm-right-don't-argue-with-me voice.

"Fine", Peter said and he slouched off.

Bath and breakfast done, the kids planned on going for a walk again but Papa said, "Maybe we can play board games at home?"

He looked so hopeful that the kids didn't want to break his heart but they really needed to find a spot for the bakery. So, Hannah said, "Sorry Papa but we need to be somewhere. How about movie night?"

Movie night was when the kids headed up to the roof to watch a movie under the starry/polluted sky of New York. Papa, with his brother's (Uncle Arthur) help had installed a projector and a big screen onto which they could project the movie. Then, Uncle Arthur had constructed fifteen Adirondack chairs and the kids had helped paint them in many vibrant colors. Mama made popcorn and each time, she added a new flavor which was pretty much the only reason the kids agreed to this.

At the mention of movie night, Papa's eyes lit up and he said, "Okay."

They took Brownie again (he whined when he saw Molly disappearing) and they went for another walk. This time, they steered clear of 50th Street but Brownie tugged on his leash and Molly, not able to hold, had to let go. He ran off and they followed him only to find him in front of that creepy, old hut again, hackles risen and tail up.

This time, they decided to investigate and approached the hut. They saw a woman in her early thirties with long, blonde hair, exploring the hut. She heard them approach and she turned around.

"Who are you?", Harry asked.

"I'm Mary Robins. I work for James Real Estate company and I thought that this place would be of use in my properties list."

"Hmm...", Hannah said, pretending to be interested. "Why though?"

"You see, there is an old story about this place. It is said that this place was one the most famous bakery in *all* of Brooklyn. It was owned by a humble family, who kept the bakery in excellent condition."

"But", Harry said. "If this bakery was in good condition, why is it like this now?"

"Ah...", Mary said. "You see, the owners had a daughter who continued operating this bakery even after her parents died. But *her* son and daughter did not want to spend their time baking for other people. They wanted to become doctors or engineers and serve other people. So, they moved abroad and they never came back, fearing that their parents might force them into running the bakery."

"Aw...", Hannah said. "Poor parents. That's just sad."

"Yes, it is", Mary said. "After the owner's daughter turned into a lady in her late seventies, she retired and never gave the bakery to anyone nor did she try to maintain the condition of the bakery. She let it fall into disrepair, already in depression about the death of her husband, who had died not a few years back before she retired. After that, rumors spread about this place being haunted by that old lady's ghost which never got to see the bakery being successfully operated by her children. It is said that the ghost roams around even to this day but I think that it is a bunch of nonsense. So, I decided to investigate for myself and all I found were a few stray rats."

"Wow", Molly said. "That's a lot of information."

"Hmm...", Anne said. Tugging on Hannah's sleeve she whispered, "I feel that this place will be perfect for Mama's bakery."

"I feel so too", Hannah whispered back. She turned to Mary and said, "If we want to buy this place, how much do you think it will cost?"

"Look", Mary said. "I don't even know *who* owns this place. How about you do me a favor and find out the actual owners of this place."

"And what do we get in return?"

"The building."

"For?"

"Let's say four thousand dollars."

The kids knew that four thousand dollars was a big amount. But when they tried to negotiate with Mary she said, "Four thousand or no site."

Desperate to build Mama's bakery, they agreed and left to the library.

"Why the library?", Molly asked. "When we have the internet?"

"Because, whichever family owned this place, they must have lived here two hundred years back. They will be mentioned in one of the library books about restaurants. See, there will hardly be two or three pieces of information on them, that's all. For that, who will take the trouble of putting them into the net?", Hannah explained.

They reached the library and all five Smith kids let the smell of books and hushed voices wash over them as they entered.

"Found it!", Peter cried after an hour of searching. "Listen to this. The Family Bakery on 50th Street, Brooklyn, New York belonged to Mr. and Mrs. Turner. 'It was the best bakery in town', a local resident had said, three years after the owners had died and the bakery fell into disrepair. 'The Family Bakery' was named so, as the owners thought that their children and grandchildren would take the responsibility of the bakery into their hands and help preserve the family legacy. However, the grandchildren moved abroad and never came back much to the disappointment of the parents. Some say it was the fear of being forced to run the bakery. Some say that the grandchildren died abroad. We never know. Four years has passed since the last owners of the bakery died and still, the building has not been claimed by anyone till now. Will Brooklyn ever get its bakery back? Or will the ghost of Mrs. Turner haunt the ruins forever?"

"Harry!", Hannah squealed suddenly, clutching his arm. "Don't you see? The *Turner* family! That means-------"

"Mike's family!", Harry said, his eyes shining with excitement. "Let me call Mike now."

Harry dialed Mike's number and they had a hushed conversation. As the call ended, Harry faced his siblings, but his face showed the disappointment.

"Says he doesn't know", Harry said. "He asked his mom and she said as far as she could remember, their family had been running a gift shop and not a bakery."

They walked back to 50th Street dejectedly and saw Mary waiting for them, fondling Brownie, who was wagging his tail.

"So", she said. "You're back."

Mary insisted that they talk over the matter through lunch and she took them to the best hotel in Brooklyn.

"It said in the library that the Turner family were the rightful owners to the bakery. We have a friend and we contacted him but he said he had no idea of the bakery whatsoever.", Harry said.

"Hmm...", Mary said. "You know, Turner is a very common surname. It could have been another family too."

Hannah looked rather sad as she said, "Maybe we're not going to buy the property after all."

"Hey", Mary said. "What a silly thought. I can still give you the place for four thousand."

They looked surprised. "But", Molly said. "You don't know who *owns* the place."

Mary waved a fork at them. "Oh, bunch of crap. I'll give it to you. But, no less than four thousand. And within three days."

After lunch, as the siblings walked back home, they discussed on how to meet the four thousand dollars demand.

"Let's check our pocket money", Anne said and everyone nodded.

They reached home and went upstairs. Everybody emptied their piggy banks and Harry added it up.

"I have five hundred dollars. Hannah has four hundred; wow that's good. Peter and Molly combined is another six hundred; okay. And that adds up to----"

"One thousand five hundred dollars", Hannah said who was quick at math.

"Harry", Anne said, tugging in his sleeve. "You forgot *my* money."

"I didn't think you had any", Harry said emptying her bank. He whistled after a minute. "Six hundred; wow that's a ***lot***."

Anne puffed up proudly. "So", she said. "What's the total?"

"Two thousand one hundred dollars", Hannah said.

"Okay", Harry said. "Well, that's a good start."

"But", Peter said. "We still have to pay her----"

"One thousand ninety dollars."

"Yeah", Peter said. "Thanks Hannah."

"No problem."

"Hey", Harry said. "We'll make ends meet. Jus—Just give me some time, that's all."

They put the money into an envelope, shoved it into Harry's drawer and went down. Mama was preparing popcorn and Fluffy was in the kitchen snoozing, lulled to sleep by the steady hum of the microwave. Every time the timer beeped, he would wake up and hiss, causing Pat to squawk, "Beep! Beep! Beep!", which would make Fluffy even *more* annoyed. Hannah peeked over her mom's shoulder and saw four bowls; classic salted, caramel, cheese and chili.

"You promised Papa movie night", Mama said, sensing Hannah. "Now pay the price."

"Whatever for?", said Peter, who had his nose pressed against the microwave door, watching the kernels pop.

"It's a horror movie", Mama said, sprinkling the cheese flavored powder on the popcorn and tossing it. Everybody groaned.

"I think I'll sit this one out", Anne said.

"Sit it out! Sit it out!", Pat said causing Papa to look into the kitchen.

"What!", he said. "Which one of you is sitting movie night *out*?"

"Now you've done it", Harry muttered. "None of us, Papa", he said, trying to sound as innocent as possible. "Anne was just *wondering* if she should."

"Well, don't", Papa said. "Cause the movie's not scary *at all.*"

Everyone rolled their eyes. They enjoyed movie night though, for as Papa had promised, the movie wasn't that scary after all. Everyone was tired after the movie was over and they went into their rooms and crashed almost immediately.

SIX

(DAYS FOR BAKERY:6)

The next morning, Mama served them bowls of fruit salad for breakfast. Anne grumbled but Mama made her eat. While Anne was separating her favorite ones (watermelon, grapes and apple) from the not so favorite fruits (starfruit, kiwi and papaya), Hannah took out the envelope and put in in her jacket pocket. Having already finished with her breakfast, she decided to call Mike and talk to him about the end of term party. She borrowed Harry's phone and their conversation went a little something like this:

Hannah: Hi Mike.

Mike: Hey. Tell me.

Hannah: So... about that party...

Mike: Yeah?

Hannah: I was thinking that it would be nice to go with you.

Mike: So... yes?

Hannah: Yeah.

Mike: Oh-yeah-that's-great-okay-see-you-later-okay-bye. ***BEEP***

Hannah: Uh... I guess?

After her call, she went down to find her siblings ready. They looked at her with anxious faces but she smiled at them reassuringly and they left.

"Wow", Mary said, opening the envelope and counting the money. "Two thousand one hundred dollars is a lot to collect in one day. I'm impressed."

Harry smiled wanly. "Yeah, but see", he said. "We need to start renovating this place. So, you need to let us work here."

Mary considered the thought for a minute. "Fine", she said. "Start tomorrow."

They thanked her and decided to visit the Turner gift and decoration shop. But Peter and Molly were tired from yesterday's movie night and they wanted to sleep. So did Anne. So, Harry offered to walk them home and Hannah decided to go alone to the shop.

As Hannah made her way to the shop, she thought about the list of items that she would need to buy. She had saved a little money (two hundred dollars to be exact) in another bank of hers. Walking inside the shop, she took a glance around and started to pile things into a box.

"I'll take these", she said, after twenty minutes, handing the box to Mike's mom.

"Hey", Mrs. Turner said. "You're Hannah, aren't you?"

"Yes Mrs. Turner. I suppose Mike told you?"

"Yeah, he did", she said. "Well, if you're having this, then it will be a hundred dollars, thank you."

Hannah went home, cradling an enormous box under her arm and found Harry waiting for her.

"I'll open this after they're awake", she said, putting the box down. "I need a nap too."

"Wood, paint, tools, streamers, balloons, glitter paper, charts, biscuits... *biscuits*?", Molly said, holding up a box of chocolate biscuits.

"Oh, that's for us", Hannah said, airily. "What do you think?"

"I think it's perfect.", Harry said. "One question, isn't your allowance five dollars?"

"Yeah?", Hannah said.

“And mine is seven.”

“So?”

“How about we do all the jobs at home and increase our allowance?”

Hannah’s eyes lit up. “So we can pay for the bakery!”, she said.

“Yeah!”, Harry said.

The whole day, Hannah and Harry worked hard and it paid off, for Mama called them to her room at the end of the day and awarded Harry ten and Hannah ten.

“Thank you!”, they said.

“Just for this week though.”

Mama had also called Peter, Molly and Anne to her room as they had helped with the chores too and totally, they had received fifteen.

“Wow”, Hannah said. “That’s thirty-five dollars. Good job everyone!”

Feeling happy, the siblings went to sleep. They felt unstoppable in this mission of conquering the spot for the bakery for Mama.

Of course, it was only until the next day, that they figured out that there was a surprise planted for them all along.

SEVEN

(DAYS FOR BAKERY:5)

The next day, the siblings planned on meeting Mary at the bakery in the morning but Mama made them stay and help her out a little bit in the kitchen.

"I have a lot of orders today", she explained. "So, I just need two hours of help."

The kids were a mess by eleven in the morning, covered from head to toe in flour so they decided to take baths, relax and visit Mary after lunch.

"Thirty-five!", Mary exclaimed. "You guys are a miracle! But one thousand eight hundred and sixty-five dollars are still left, you know?"

"Yeah", Harry said. "And you want the money by tomorrow."

"It's fine. You guys get on with the refurbishing."

Harry called Uncle Arthur and asked him to come over. They spent all morning and afternoon working on the bakery and it was done by three o' clock in the afternoon.

"Well", Uncle Arthur said, helping them pack up. "No telling your mom, is it?"

"Mm hmm. No telling Papa either."

"Okay", he said and he left.

"Good job", Mary said. "Make sure you get the money tomorrow."

"The document is sent", Harry said.

They had done some research and they had found out that they had to send a document to the Health and Sanitation Department containing the blueprints of the bakery.

"When will the reply come?", Molly asked.

"Tomorrow. Along with the investigators."

"What for?", Peter asked.

"To check whether the blueprints match the bakery, right Hannah?", Molly asked.

"Yes Molly", Hannah said, sounding surprised. "I'm proud of you. You're learning fast."

"She learns from the best", Harry said, proudly puffing his chest out. Everyone laughed as Hannah rolled her eyes.

"Alright", Hannah said. "Let's get a move on and get some work done."

They worked for the rest of the day, helping their parents in household chores and they were rewarded with twenty for both Harry and Hannah and twenty-five for Anne, Molly and Peter.

"Forty-five", Harry said, yawning. "Is not bad. So that leaves us with----"

"One thousand eight hundred and twenty", Hannah said. "Just so you know, I have two hundred dollars left over from the shopping I did. So, actually *one thousand six hundred and twenty.*"

"We still need to pay it to her though", Peter said.

"Oh, I'll negotiate something. Loss of business for her too, actually, if we don't agree to buy the site."

"Okay", Molly said. "I don't want to sleep now. Can we play Monopoly?"

Two hours later, Anne was rolling in cash, Harry was bankrupt and Peter and Hannah were sick of staring at the board.

"I QUIT!", Peter said, flinging his money down. "I'm going to sleep."

"Yeah", Harry said, getting to his feet. "Me too."

"Come on", Hannah said, pulling the notes out of Molly's hand who protested. "We've had a long day. Let's get some rest, okay?"

Hannah packed the game and put it back in its place. Then she made sure that the pets were asleep and ushered her two sisters back into the room and slept.

Nobody noticed the loud meowing and hissing along with the squawks that followed it in the middle of the night for everyone slept like a pile of logs.

They had only noticed, when Anne had been the first to wake up the next morning to find that her beloved parrot was lying dead on the living room carpet and that both Queenie's and Fluffy's fur was stained with red blood.

EIGHT

(DAYS FOR BAKERY:4)

"MAMA!!", Anne sobbed, burying her face with both her hands and a mass of hair. "PAT is DEAD!"

Mama came down the stairs, her hair a mess followed by Papa and the rest of the kids. They saw Pat motionless on the living room carpet and Queenie's and Fluffy's fur red.

Anne was sobbing until Mama went up to her and pulled her into a hug. They all crowded round their youngest sibling as she cried and cried and cried until all her tears had been exhausted.

"Queenie and Fluffy killed Pat", Peter said causing Anne to burst into fresh tears. Harry, Hannah, Papa and Mama glared at him.

"What?", he said. "I only spoke the truth. Look at their fur."

They all gazed closely at Fluffy and Queenie and saw that their fur *was* red. Harry and Hannah volunteered to clean the cats as Peter and Molly helped Anne calm down.

Hannah and Harry, done with cleaning the cats came out of the bathroom and Hannah said, "Go on. I need something from my room."

She went to her room only to find an envelope on the table with six hundred dollars nestled inside. Shocked, she turned the envelope over and saw a note that said, **"All The Best."**

Cradling the envelope as though it was made of gold, Hannah went down to her siblings and called a quick meeting. The left Mama, who was organizing a burial for Pat and went to the DR.

"Six hundred dollars!", Harry exclaimed. "Who would do that?"

"I don't know", Hannah said. "But we owe them a lot."

"You bet we do", Harry said, grinning.

The siblings packed that money along with the remaining forty-five dollars and got ready to leave for the bakery. Just as they were about to head out the door, Anne squealed.

"WAIT!", she said. "I've forgotten something." She ran upstairs and came back with a twenty dollar note.

"I had kept this in my boot. Granny gave it last year for my birthday." Stowing that too in the envelope, the Smiths left to the bakery. When they got there, they saw that the Health and Sanitation Department had arrived and were checking the bakery under Mary's supervision.

"Hey", Hannah said handing Mary the envelope. Mary rifled through the notes and said, "One thousand two hundred dollars are pending. You said you'd pay by today."

"Sorry", Harry said. "We'll get it tomorrow. You see our pet parrot------"

"You said today. You promised.", Mary said, her eyes narrowing. The people from the department handed Hannah a file containing the approved documents and they left.

"Yeah", Harry said, anger rising within him. "But our pet----"

"Can I see that?", Mary said, reaching out for the documents. Hannah handed it over as a black car pulled over.

"Sorry", Mary said. "But business is business. Don't mix it up with your personal problems." Saying that, she got into the car and it sped off.

The five kids stared after her.

"No way!", Peter said.

"Cheat", Molly said.

"Unempathetic human", Harry said.

Anne burst into tears again and Hannah carried her home as her siblings wordlessly followed.

After they reached home, Anne was given the task of working on the bakery's sign and they had a quick meeting to decide the name and they finalized on 'Sweet Tooth.'

One good thing that came out of it was that it kept Anne busy for the rest of the day as the other siblings helped Mama clean Pat up.

At the end of the day, Anne was done with a beautiful sign that would have been worthy of the bakery, only if they had gotten the site.

"Wow Anne", Peter said. "That looks amazing!"

"Thanks", Anne said, obviously pleased with her work. The sign was complete with drawings and words adjusted perfectly in the exact size. Anne enlisted the help of her siblings to color it in and by dinnertime, the sign was done.

Dinner was light, being homemade pizza for a change and after they were done eating, the siblings went silently up to their rooms, not having anything to discuss, each one of them weighing the loss of the bakery that they had dreamed of.

NINE

The next morning, was a bright one with a pinkish-blue sky sleeping against the brick-red buildings in the bustling city of New York. Hannah, however, was more blue than bright that morning and didn't move till Fluffy peed on her bed.

"FLUFFY!", Hannah said, not knowing whether to laugh or scold. "WHAT were you thinking? BAD CAT!!"

Fluffy didn't mind even though it meant he had to be slapped by Hannah for what he had done. He went down the stairs to find Mama waiting for him, an eyebrow raised at the commotion that had happened upstairs.

"Mm-kay?", Mama said.

"Meow!", Fluffy said, indignantly. "ME-OW!"

"Yeah, right", she said, and heading to the kitchen. When she saw Fluffy following, she turned around and said, "SHOO!"

After breakfast, everyone dressed in black for Pat's burial. At ten o'clock sharp, they got into their car and drove off.

Mama had invited their family members, Mr. Roberts and Mrs. Sandy (their upstairs neighbors) and many friends for the burial. Surprisingly, everybody had showed up. Anne had also been surprised with the arrival of her best friend, Jenny along with her pet cat, Tuxedo.

"Hey Anne", Jenny said. "I got Tuxedo."

"Yeah", Anne said, sadly. "She can play with Queenie?"

"Okay", said Jenny and not wanting to push it, left. Then, Mr. Roberts arrived.

"Mr. Roberts", Anne sobbed, burying her head into his coat. "I feel so alone." Mr. Roberts was like a grandfather figure to the five Smiths.

"Anne", he said, speaking in his deep voice. "One loses things all the time." Then, looking at her condition, he said, "It's okay. Come, we'll go hear the speech."

After the burial, the Smiths had organized a lunch in the church ground. The lunch included fried chicken, macaroni and cheese, bread, salad, pizza, cakes, ice cream and ginger beer for those who wanted it.

The Smiths went home dejectedly and Mama called a family meeting.

"Look", she said, cupping Anne's chin. "Everything has its own lifeline. You can't prevent anything. Pat would have died anyway due to old age." When Anne didn't respond, she said, "I'll buy you a hamster. How about that?"

Anne's face lost half its sorrow as she said, "Really?"

"Yes." They sat in silence for five minutes, each Smith swallowing the loss they had faced. The day took a better turn, only for Hannah though as the doorbell rang, startling everyone.

"I'll get it", Harry said. Opening the door, he said, "Oh! Hi Mike!"

Hannah looked up in surprise. "Mike?", she said.

"Hi Harry", Mike said. Looking at Hannah and then at Mama, he said, "Mrs. Smith... would it be okay if I took your daughter out?"

Mama nodded. "If she approves. And be back before nightfall."

Mike looked at Hannah and she nodded, smiling reluctantly.

While Hannah and Mike were out, Mama decided to take Anne out for her pet hamster shopping. At the store, Anne picked the cutest, fluffiest and cuddliest hamster she could find.

"Okay", said Mama, as she drove back home, one hour later, Anne nuzzling the furry little thing. "Happy?"

"Yeah... no. I mean, I miss Pat but she's kinda replacing him for me."

"She?"

"Yeah. The pet store guy told me that this one is a she."

Mama shook her head, resigned. "Well, what are you going to name her?"

"Petunia or Diana or Cutie.", Anne said. "Or maybe I'll decide with Molly and Peter."

"Have fun. Although, I do hope you pick a sensible name for her. Remember, it needs to be------"

"Short, sweet and easy to pronounce", Anne said, having heard this sentence many a times before.

They burst into laughter and the hamster squeaked loudly, sending bouts of warmth and love through Anne.

"The movies?", Hannah said, as Mike asked the cab driver to pull up in front of a cinema hall. "Mike, a café would have been okay, you know?"

Mike smiled, rather mischievously. "So... you want to go back?"

"No", Hannah said, hurriedly and let herself be pulled inside the hall.

An hour and a half later, Mike and Hannah were out of the hall, the movie done.

"So", Mike said. "How was it?"

"Wow", Hannah said. "That's all that I can say. Wow!"

"So, where to next?"

Harry was feeling bored at home. Papa had some work to do and Molly and Peter were fussing over Brownie. So, he called his friends and left for a basketball match. His phone, a gift from his aunt and uncle on his twelfth birthday, came in very useful in such situations, which prevented him from running around his parents whenever he wanted to make a call. The others were often scorned at by him, which they did not like very much.

Walking onto the basketball court he saw Oliver (Molly's best friend), John, Daniel and a few of his other school friends. They split up into teams and commenced playing.

After an hour of proper workout, Harry sat on the court's bench and thought about how to approach Jane on the party's matter. So lost in thought he was that he didn't see Hannah and Mike until Hannah pinched him on the shoulder.

"OW!", he exclaimed, rubbing the exact spot where Hannah had pinched him. "Sorry, but... I need to go to Jane's. I figured something out, I think. Bye!" And he walked off.

Mike stared at Hannah. "You think he's got this?"

Hannah shook her head. "He'll be back."

And sure enough, there was Harry. "Can you guys come?"

Hannah smiled knowingly at Mike and they left.

"Diana sounds good", Peter said, playing a small game of hypnotizing his rabbits with pieces of carrots. PB snatched the piece of carrot that Peter was holding, causing him to groan. "Aw man!", he said, looking at PB. "That's the third wand you've swallowed today."

PB looked at him innocently and Jelly (J) twitched her nose. Then she squeaked, causing the hamster to shudder at the pitch.

"Yeah", Molly said, stroking J to calm her down. "Diana sounds good."

"Fine then", Anne said. "Diana it is."

She went down to tell Mama and in two minutes, they could hear her yapping away.

"Good old Anne", Molly said. "What with the failed bakery and Pat's death, that poor thing's been through a lot."

"Well, she's stronger than any of us.", Peter said. "Any other six-year-old would have cried themselves to bits. She's strong."

"Hi Jane!", Hannah said, walking into Jane's room. Jane's mother, Mrs. Hope, had let them in.

"Hey Hannah", Jane said, smiling and standing up to hug Hannah. Catching sight of Mike, she asked, "Need any advice?"

Hannah laughed. "No. Actually, my brother wants to talk to you."

Jane's smile vanished. "Who? Peter? I haven't seen him in a while, you know."

"No again", Hannah said. "*Harry* wants to talk."

Jane's face darkened as Harry stepped out from behind Hannah and said, "Hey!"

"What?", Jane snapped.

"Can we talk?"

"NO!"

Harry's temper rose. "What!", he yelled. "What is your PROBLEM?!"

Jane was seething with anger as she said, "YOU are the problem!!"

"Fine!", Harry said, boiling with rage. "Just go to------- forget it."

They watched as he stormed out of the room. Mike went after him and Hannah turned to Jane.

"What was that?", she asked, quietly.

"Hannah", Jane snapped. "Leave me alone."

Hannah was quite short-tempered and didn't usually tolerate any remarks or orders of the sort except when it came from her elders. Her temper rising, she said, "You will regret it if I walk out of this room, Jane."

"Hannah, I----", Jane said but Hannah shook her head.

"Stop. Just one last question."

"Fine", Jane said.

"What happened between you two?"

"We were really good friends", Jane began. "We had so much fun together in the holidays when you used to go for your piano classes. We used to play together and... we were like siblings. But one day, we were playing football and I was hardly five at that time. I tripped and fell and I started to bleed. My hands and knees were cut. It felt like my ankle was sprained too. Mike was there at that time... you can ask him. Anyway, I couldn't bear the pain and I started to cry. Harry was used to playing rough at that time and he was quite strong. But instead of helping me up, he criticized me and called me weak and said that if I was really strong, I should get up and play. I looked at Mike for help but he stood next to Harry and told me that I should have strengthened myself before playing with boys. Although, I knew he didn't mean it at that time as he only said that after Harry glared at him for reaching his hand out. So", Jane said, pausing for breath. "You know now what happened."

"Oh", Hannah said. "I never knew. I'm sorry Jane, I should have never spoken to you like that."

"It's ok."

They sat in silence for a minute.

"Well", Hannah said. "I think it's best I tell you why we were here."

"Go on."

"Harry wanted to ask you out to the end of term party in our school."

"No way!"

"Yeah. Just... talk to him, ok? And make sure you guys clear things out before going together."

Jane smiled. "I will. And tell him that I might call him tomorrow."

"Sure."

There was an awkward moment of silence and then Hannah said, "Well... bye."

"Bye."

Hannah walked home and thought about the past few days and reflected on them. She felt mixed; happy that Jane and Harry were going to get fixed; sad about Mama's failed bakery; excited for Mama's birthday and for her and Mike and concerned for her siblings. Her thoughts relaxed as she reached home but immediately was greeted by the tensed looks of her siblings as she stepped inside.

TEN

"What?", Hannah asked.

"We have a problem", Harry said.

"Okay?"

"Anne might have messed up."

"What do you mean?"

"I spoke to Mr. Roberts", Anne blurted out. "By accident though."

Hannah took this in slowly. "Spoke to Mr. Roberts about what?"

"About the bakery."

Hannah's eyes widened. "You did not."

"Accident!", Anne grimaced.

"Talk me through *exactly* what you told him."

"Okay", Anne said. "It went like this..."

i. ***The conversation between Anne and Mr. Roberts.***

- ***Location:*** *At Mr. Roberts' house.*
- ***Topic:*** *Mama's failed bakery.*
- ***Time:*** *When Hannah, Harry and Mike were at Jane's.*

"Hi Mr. Roberts", Anne said.

"Hi Anne. Good to see you", Mr. Roberts said in his deep voice. "What brings you here? Is it about Pat?"

"No. I just came up here to see you. Where is Mrs. Sandy?"

"She's gone out to by some groceries."

"Ah."

"There is something on your mind, Anne", Mr. Roberts said. "Tell me what it is."

And that's when Anne poured it out. All the feelings that she had been holding since the past few days. She told Mr. Roberts everything; how Mary had taken so much money and how she had taken away the documents suddenly. How they had felt cheated after so much of work since Pat's death had come up so suddenly too. Mr. Roberts listened attentively and didn't interrupt. When she was done, he let out a deep breath.

"Well, you've been through a lot, young lady."

"I know Mr. Roberts. I just wish we could do something about it."

"Maybe I can", Mr. Roberts said, his eyes twinkling.

Anne left and it was only as she entered her room that she realized she had spoken to Mr. Roberts about the bakery. Hearing Harry at the door, she had gone down and immediately informed him about what had happened.

Now, Hannah stared at her, dumbstruck as Anne finished her story.

"Great", Hannah said, sarcastically. "God knows what he'll do now."

"I hope it's not bad", Peter said, stroking Fluffy, who was in his arms.

"It won't be", Molly assured him. Everybody stared at her in surprise.

"How are you so sure?", Harry asked.

"Because I know that Mr. Roberts is a *good* man."

"Well", Hannah said. "The outcome of this... escapade better be good. Or else, Anne knows what she has to do, I hope."

"I do", Anne said, flatly. "Penance. And it's not sweet."

"Well, I'm glad you realized that.", Hannah said. "Come on, I think Mama's calling us for dinner."

Dinner was spaghetti and meatballs which lifted everyone's spirits. As they ate, they discussed Mama's birthday.

"We're planning a surprise", Papa said, winking at the kids who winked back.

"Tell me", Mama pleaded. "I'm begging to know."

"Ah", Papa said, mischievously. "That's the *surprise.*"

Mama rolled her eyes. "It better be good."

"You sound like Hannah", Molly said.

"Actually", Mama said. "Hannah sounds like me!"

"Well", Harry said. "The part of your birthday which is not a surprise is your trip to the movies and lunch with Papa."

"Expected", Mama said, shrugging. They all laughed and as they snuggled into their blankets after dinner, they felt happier than ever in their lives.

ELEVEN

The next morning, the Smiths woke up on time and got ready, for Mama had planned on going birthday shopping. After breakfast (sausages and bread with egg), they hopped into the car and they left.

"What kind of dress are you going to buy Mama?", Anne asked.

"Um... I've not decided yet."

"Well, Hannah, Molly and I are always there to help you out."

"Thanks honey. That means a lot."

They spent the entire morning shopping and Mama settled for a sleeveless, flowery purple gown with a pink overcoat to go on top.

"Wow", Molly said, as they drove back home. "That dress is gorgeous!"

"You helped me select it", Mama said, her face flushed with happiness.

"Yeah", Molly said, puffing her chest out. "We did."

"Your birthday is tomorrow, right?", Peter said. "Or is it the day after tomorrow?"

"Tomorrow", Mama said. "Honestly Peter! That's the only thing we've been talking about for days!"

They went home and slept in the afternoon, tuckered out with all the shopping they had done. They woke up at four-thirty in the evening.

"Mr. Roberts had called", Harry said, checking his phone after he washed his face. "I don't know why."

"Call him back later", Peter said, who shared a room with Harry. "Mama's calling us for tea."

"It could be important", Harry implored as they joined their sisters.

"What could?", Hannah asked.

"Mr. Roberts' call."

"Actually... Harry, after tea, we need to plan Mama's surprise. I mean, the last few bits need to be fixed. Mama's going out with one of her friends to a baking exhibition and we have at least three hours before she comes back and says *'BEDTIME!'*"

"Oh", Harry said. "Right. I'll text him. It can wait."

But what Harry didn't know, was that that call, was very, very important, especially for the kids, as it was regarding the very bakery that they had planned to give their mother.

Anyway, the kids had fun, planning the surprises for Mama's *surprise* birthday party.

"Surprise cake, surprise breakfast-in-bed, surprise family visit, surprise pet talent show and surprise gift", Molly said. "The gift will come with Uncle Arthur, right?"

"Yeah", Papa said.

The surprise gift was supposed to be a wooden wall hanging in the shape of a heart with all the six Smith family members' names surrounding Mama's name.

"Good", Hannah said. "Then we don't need to conduct this meeting beyond this point."

Anne let out a huge yawn and so did Peter.

"Up you get", Hannah said. "I'll put you to bed and sleep myself. Boy, am I tired."

After Hannah left with Peter and Anne, Harry said, "Papa?"

"Yes?"

"Whatever happened to the bakery?"

Papa hesitated and said, "We actually *weren't* able to find any good... spots."

"Hmm...", Molly said. "So, you will not get a bakery?"

Papa stood up. "I'm sorry Molly. But we did a lot of research and we still couldn't find any good places. I'm sorry if I got your hopes up but... it will not happen. Not this time, anyway." Saying that, he went to his room.

"I feel bad", Molly said.

Harry put his arm around her and Molly felt loved and safe for a sudden moment.

"I know", he said. "I only wish we could have gotten that bakery."

"Me too.", Molly said.

She hugged her brother tightly and said, "Even though we couldn't get the bakery, I feel happy that I still have you guys."

Harry hugged her back and kissed her on the forehead. Then he stood up, took Molly to her room, tucked her in and went to his room to get a good night's sleep.

Nobody heard Mama come back that night, moving the couch a little bit, shuffling the chairs and opening the cabinets looking for signs of a hidden surprise like a badger on a night prowl looking for food. Nobody stirred as she crept into the rooms and secretly kissed them goodnight.

TWELVE

Harry was the first to wake the next morning. He felt a sudden bout of energy in his veins and wondered why. Then he realized that it was Mama's birthday and he leapt out of bed in joy. Shaking Peter awake, he walked into the girls' room and shook them awake too.

"Harry!", mumbled Hannah, trying to swat at him as though he was a fly. "What is the matter?"

"It's Mama's birthday! Wake up before she does!"

Right on cue, Papa stepped into the room.

"Ready?", he asked. Then, looking at the girls he said, "Aw... You're not even awake. No cake for you guys."

At that sentence, all three girls leaped out of bed and ran to the bathroom.

"Huh", Papa said to Harry as he closed the room door. "It's amazing what cake can do."

Harry chuckled. The Smith kids then spent the next hour preparing Mama's surprise; Hannah, Papa and Molly worked on the breakfast, Harry and Peter made sure the cake and pets were ready and Anne was outside her parents' bedroom, attentively listening for signs that let her know when Mama was awake.

They finished on time for just as Harry coaxed Fluffy into hiding beneath his spot under the couch and the trio in the kitchen finished with the breakfast, Anne said, "Quick! I can hear her!"

They arranged Mama's breakfast onto a plate and Peter gave Anne a thumbs-up. She went into the room and two seconds later, they heard Mama squeal excitedly. Anne came out and gave them the all-clear sign.

"Good to go", Harry said. Hannah ran into the basement and they heard the piano coming to life.

Papa took the plate followed by Harry, Peter, Molly and Anne. As they entered the room, they began to sing 'Happy Birthday' accompanied by Hannah's piano downstairs. Mama teared up and she said, "Oh! It's lovely dearies. Thank you so much."

They let her eat breakfast in peace and Papa let her get dressed for her movie. The kids were to be left at home; a usual tradition on *Mama's birthday only*. After Mama and Papa left, the kids sat down contentedly on the couch and suddenly, Harry's phone buzzed.

"Ugh!", he exclaimed. "That's the twentieth missed call I am getting from Mr. Roberts from yesterday."

Hannah's brow furrowed. "Call him back", she said. Harry dialed Mr. Roberts and he put it on speaker.

"Hello Mr. Roberts", they chorused.

"Hello kids. Harry, why didn't you pick my call?"

"I'm sorry Mr. Roberts, we were a little preoccupied. You see, our mom's birthday is today so...", he trailed off.

"It's okay", Mr. Roberts said. "Actually, this--- I mean, *these* calls were regarding your mother's bakery. Anne informed me of this and------ could it be possible for you to come upstairs? We could talk face-to-face."

"Yeah", Molly said. And they went upstairs.

"You did what?", Anne said. "Mr. Roberts, how is that even possible?"

Mr. Roberts had just informed the Smiths that he had fired Mary Robins and had had her arrested for bribing too.

"I am the head of that particular branch. And the employees there are *my* responsibility. So... I fired her. Besides, that property was only worth three thousand. The extra thousand was a bribe from her end."

The kids gasped as Mrs. Sandy hollered, "LUNCH!", from the kitchen.

After lunch which was pasta, the kids sat with Mr. Roberts again.

"So...", Harry said. "Do we get the property back?"

"What do you think, Harry?", Mr. Roberts asked, his eyes twinkling. "Do you want it or not?"

"We do", Peter replied. Then it dawned on him and he said, "You're actually giving it to us!?"

The others stared at Mr. Roberts as he slowly pulled out a file, nodding. He handed it out to Hannah, who took it, speechless.

"I--- thank--- thank you!", she stammered. "We owe you a lot."

"Well", Mr. Roberts said, mischief playing in his eyes. "I think you have only an hour and a half to get your mother to the bakery. You have to get her there by dusk or the surprise will be ruined."

The kids got up and hugged Mr. Roberts. Then they raced downstairs, each Smith kid overwhelmed with happiness about the dream bakery.

THIRTEEN

"Get the sign!", Hannah hissed to Anne who immediately scampered off in search of it.

"Where are we going?", Mama asked, observing them pack. Molly squealed.

"Mama!", she said, shooing her out of the room. "It's TOP SECRET!"

Twenty minutes later they were done.

Five minutes later they left the house. Harry called all his family members and Mama's friends and asked them to come to 50th Street.

Ten minutes it took for them to arrive at 50th Street, at a spot just a little further than the bakery.

Six minutes it took for them to help their Uncle Arthur fix the signboard and cover it with a sheet as the rest of the family members and friends kept an eye on Mama.

Forty-five minutes since they left the house. Forty-five more minutes to go. The kids spent another half hour decorating the bakery to its full extent. Finally, they led Mama and Papa over to the bakery, their eyes blindfolded.

"What is it?", Mama asked, unable to bear the suspense any longer. "Something that will make me ground you?"

"No"

"Something that will make me sad?"

"NO!"

"Something that will make me want to dance?"

"Kind of", Hannah said. "Harry, remove Papa's blindfold. And Papa, do **not** tell Mama what you see."

Papa nearly, *very nearly* screamed out loud when he saw the bakery. He turned to his five kids, his eyes filled with happy tears and cried when he saw them nod. Hannah uncovered her mom's eyes and Mama let out a stifled scream.

"The bakery! Oh my god, how did you guys do this?"

"Surprise!", the kids yelled.

To their horror, they saw tears roll down their mom's face.

"I'm shocked", Mama said, waving her kids away. "That's all."

After the excitement calmed down, the kids uncovered the sign to reveal the name of the bakery, one which they had already decided on before finding a plot. As Mama saw the sign, her eyes widened and she said, "The Sweet Tooth! Oh! John...", she said, turning to Papa. "Didn't we decide on the same name?"

Papa nodded, unable to believe his eyes. Mama went inside the bakery to inspect it, accompanied by Papa. Meanwhile...

"We never found out who gave us the mysterious six hundred dollars, did we Harry?", Hannah asked.

"No, we didn't."

Uncle Arthur, standing behind them grinned.

"We really owe that person.", Hannah said. Turning around to look at her uncle who quickly suppressed his grin, she said, "What do you think we can do?"

"Well", he said, grin back on. "Maybe you can remember their birthday this year."

Harry's eyes widened, for they always forgot to wish Uncle Arthur on his birthday, and he said, "It was *you*!"

"Yes of course.", Uncle Arthur said.

"But why?"

"Cause I knew how hard you were working for the money. So I spoke to your Auntie Jennifer and we decided to pile six hundred; three from her end and three from mine."

"Wow!", Hannah said. "Thanks Uncle Arthur. You're a peach."

Uncle Arthur shrugged as Mama came out with Papa and said, "It's exactly as we had imagined. Thank you so much dearies."

The Smiths went home and Mama was yet again surprised by the amazing talent show done by the pets that included a back flip by Brownie, gymnastics by the two cats, dancing by the rabbits, hide-n-seek by Dory and cuddles from Diana.

Mama, later that day, when asked, had rated this the best birthday of her life.

That night, the Smiths organized a party in their house and were delighted by the arrival of all their friends, family and neighbors who had been invited. As the party slowly cleared, everyone going home, the Smiths' friends were allowed to stay for a sleepover. That meant Jane, Mike, Oliver and Jenny. Jane, Mike, Hannah and Harry decided to sleep in one room and headed upstairs to talk while Molly, Peter and Oliver sat down to play with PB and J as Anne showcased Diana's skills to Jenny.

"How does Anne cope with you guys?", Oliver asked.

"What do you mean?", Peter asked. "She has like... three pets man. How can she *not*? Especially when one of them is not trained."

As if to prove that point, Diana came running at top speed and flung herself onto Oliver who fell backwards. The just as he sat up, Anne was in his lap and Diana gone.

"Uh...", Oliver said. "You're----"

"Yeah, yeah", Anne said. "I know."

And she scampered off. Two seconds later, they heard Papa yelling.

"ANNE! Take this hamster out of my bed! I am ***not***sleeping with hamster fur and pee all over my bed."

Oliver chuckled. "Yeah, I see."

Mama called, asking the trio and Anne and Jenny to head upstairs to bed. Oliver and Jenny entered the room, leaving Mama out with her three younger kids. Each of them wished her goodnight, along with a birthday hug and went inside to sleep.

And just there, nestled in that cozy brownstone on 57th Street was the Smith family. Being the first ones to bring a smile on the faces of everybody who met them, they were adored and loved by all. The perfect combination of love, friendship and trust is what makes this family special. The one routine of fun, friendship, family and frolic is seen throughout the adventures of the siblings. Till then, we will continue to cherish the happy moments that we share with 'The Smiths of 57th Street.'

Epilogue

It was a November morning. A cold wintry snap had settled in the city making it nearly impossible for anyone to want to get out of their houses except for that one black limousine that pulled over at the brownstone on 57th Street.

Mike, a teenage boy and close friends of the Smith siblings, stepped out of the car in a suit, holding a bouquet of pink, yellow and purple pansies. He walked up to the door and rang the bell. Hannah Smith, the second of the Smith siblings, opened the door, dressed in a light-yellow gown. Trying to tie her hair, she said, "Mama! Mike's here! I'm leaving."

"Okay", came the reply, as Rebecca Smith, mother to the five Smith kids, snapped some pictures of Mike and Hannah together on Mike's phone before saying goodbye.

Having successfully tied her hair, Hannah slipped her hand into Mike's and they left for the end-of-term party in their school.

Mama, who had gone up to fetch her phone, came down two minutes after Hannah and Mike had left and saw her youngest kid, Anne, sitting on the windowsill, her nose pressed against the glass. Mama chuckled to herself as Harry, the eldest of the siblings, came down the stairs.

"Mama", Harry said, picking up his bouquet and slipping on his boots. "Can we go? I don't want to keep Jane waiting."

Jane, a friend of Hannah's, had been asked to the party by Harry. After Jane and Hannah had had that conversation, Harry had called Jane and they had spent an hour talking and fixing stuff.

"Sure honey", Mama said. She was to drive them to their school.

They left and arrived at Jane's house, not too far from their brownstone. Harry got out as Mama pulled the car over and went up to the door. Before he could ring the bell, it opened and a slim girl with blonde hair, wearing a black gown with silver frills, opened the door.

Mama watched from the car as the two exchanged words and smiled to herself as they got into the car.

My kids grew up so fast! she thought as she drove the car past the brownstone and towards their school.

Molly and Peter, the twins in the family, watched as Mama's car sped past their brownstone.

"Ugh!", Peter said. "Those parties! With those dances and talking and----", he began but Molly clamped a hand over his mouth.

"Shh...", she said. "Don't bother. They have their own likes and dislikes. Let us enjoy *our childhood* before *that* spoils everything."

www.ingramcontent.com/pod-product-compliance
Lightning Source LLC
LaVergne TN
LVHW041251150826
845673LV00008B/2538

* 9 7 9 8 8 9 6 7 3 6 5 4 7 *